Karen McCombie is the bestselling author of the *Indie Kidd* series, as well as other fiction for children and teenagers. She used to write for magazines *J17* and *Sugar*. Karen lives in London with her husband, small daughter and two fat cats.

❀ ❁ ❀

Lydia Monks won the Smarties Prize for *I Wish I Were a Dog*. She has illustrated many poetry, novelty and picture books for children, including the *Girl Zone* series for Walker. Lydia lives in Sheffield with her husband and daughter.

For Rachel Petrie, because
it's only fair! KMcC

❋ ❉ ❋

This is a work of fiction. Names, characters, places and incidents are
either the product of the author's imagination or, if real, are used fictitiously.

First published 2005 by Walker Books Ltd
87 Vauxhall Walk, London SE11 5HJ

This edition published 2007

2 4 6 8 10 9 7 5 3 1

Text © 2005 Karen McCombie
Illustrations © 2005 Lydia Monks

The right of Karen McCombie and Lydia Monks to be identified as author
and illustrator respectively of this work has been asserted by them in accordance
with the Copyright, Designs and Patents Act 1988

This book has been typeset in Granjon

Printed and bound in Great Britain by
Creative Print and Design (Wales), Ebbw Vale

British Library Cataloguing in Publication Data:
a catalogue record for this book is available from the British Library

ISBN 978-1-4063-0718-4

www.walkerbooks.co.uk

Oops, I Lost My Best(est) Friends

KAREN McCOMBIE

LYDIA MONKS

WALKER BOOKS
AND SUBSIDIARIES
LONDON · BOSTON · SYDNEY · AUCKLAND

Dylan's sorry, sad secret

There had been an explosion of gerbils.

Not a

crash

BANG

wallop

kind of explosion; a 'population explosion', that's what Mum called it.

Basically, that meant that loads of gerbils had been handed in to the *Paws For Thought* Animal Rescue Centre where she

worked, and they'd all had *heaps* of babies.
There'd been so many litters of gerbils
born that they'd run out of space to keep
them all. Which was why we had a cage

full of gerbils plonked on our kitchen worktop right now.

"How many babies *are* there, Mrs Kidd?" asked my bestest friend Soph.

"Six in this litter," Mum replied.

"How old are they?" asked Fee, peering at the snuffly, pink blobs in the straw.

Fee is my other bestest friend. Soph and Fee came round after school today to work on the poems our teacher asked us to write. Instead, we were staring at the newest foster pets in our house.

'Cause of Mum's job, we often have foster pets here, and some of them end up becoming PROPER pets, like Dibbles the not-very-pretty-but-totally-adorable dog did not so long ago.

"They're only a few hours old," I told Fee. "They were born this morning, weren't they, Mum?"

"Yes, Indie, that's right. Oh dear … it is worrying," Mum sighed.

"Why's it worrying?" asked Dylan.

Dylan is my step-brother. He hadn't 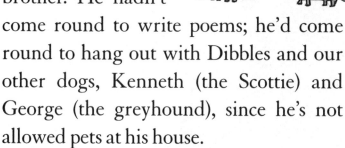 come round to write poems; he'd come round to hang out with Dibbles and our other dogs, Kenneth (the Scottie) and George (the greyhound), since he's not allowed pets at his house.

"Well, Dylan, it's worrying because it's going to be *very* hard to find homes for all these little guys!" Mum said.

Mum was so caught up in worrying that she'd totally forgotten she'd scrunched her hair into a *(sort of)* bun and *(sort of)* fixed it in place with a pencil – a pencil with a green-haired, rubber gonk on the end.

"Right, I must make a note of the gerbils' feeding rota!" she mumbled, heading out of the kitchen. "Now, where did I leave my pencil…?"

"Oooh, Indie – those babies are just the *cutest* thing!" cooed Soph, once Mum had left the room.

"Yes, I know," I said, thinking that Soph was so close to the cage that her breath must have felt like a warm breeze to the gerbil babies.

"Urgh! Are you kidding?" Fee laughed. "They look like slugs with noses!"

"Oh, yeah, Fee? Well, *you* look more like a slug with a nose than *they* do!" Soph burst out.

"I do *not*!"

"Yes, you do!" Soph insisted with a big

cheeky grin. "Then again ... you look more like a slug in a *wig*!"

Fee did a big gasp then, pretending to be hurt, though she wasn't really.

"If *I* look like a slug in a wig, Sophie Musyoka, then *you* look like a ... a ... a daddy long legs in a hoodie!"

Now that they'd both started to get silly, I wasn't sure what they'd come up with next – something dumb about me being like a bluebottle with bunches, maybe?

But then a car horn went HONK! outside, waking our cat Smudge up from her snoozles for a whole nanosecond.

"That'll be my dad," said Soph, as Smudge's eyelids started drooping and she carried on with her snooozles in the laundry basket. "Want a lift, Fee?"

"Def'nitely," said Fee, handing Soph's school bag to her.

And with a wave and a wiggle of fingers, they were both gone.

"Indie, is it hygenic to have those gerbils in the kitchen?" asked

Dylan all of a sudden, his eyes fixed on the cage.

Trust Dylan to think about stuff that no other boy of nine would think about. *Other* boys of nine might want to know *when* the baby gerbils would open their eyes, or *what* baby-gerbil poo looks like, or *if* it would be all right to feed them Quavers, but not Dylan.

"*Course* it's hygenic – this bit of the kitchen isn't where we cook or anything!" I said, while I quickly elbowed a plate of half-finished toast under a newspaper.

"How come they do that thing?"

"How come *who* do *what* thing?" I asked, thrown by Dylan's new direction in our conversation.

"Soph and Fee. How can they be horrible to each other, when they're supposed to be friends?

"But that's what friends do, isn't it?" I said with a shrug, scratching Dibbles' head as he nuzzled up and started licking my knee (he's a dog of very little brain). "Friends can just have a laugh and tease each other. It doesn't *mean* anything! Don't you do that with *your* bestest friends?"

"I don't really have any bestest friends."

When Dylan said that, I felt as stunned as if Dibbles had dropped a certificate in my lap, showing he was a qualified helicopter pilot.

"But what about at school, Dylan –
you've got to have friends at school!"

"Not really. I mean, I talk to people and
stuff, but I don't have bestest friends – not
like you and Soph and Fee."

Urgh, that made me feel sorry and sad
and kind of

WOBBLY

around the edges.

"Can you show me
how to get friends, Indie?"

Double URGH – I felt as

sorry

and
sad

and

WOBBLY

as a blackcurrant jelly now!

"Of *course* I'll help you get some friends!"

Suddenly, I wanted to give Dylan a hug, but

a) Dibbles was in the way, AND

b) I thought I might frighten Dylan.

He's not a hugging kind of boy.

But huggable or not, I knew I'd do everything I could to help my ace little (step) brother get a friend.

"It's not a proper word, y'know, Indie."

"Huh? What isn't?"

"'Bestest'," said Dylan, blinking wide-eyed at me. "You're just meant to say 'best friend', 'cause 'bestest' isn't a proper word."

Sigh.

Sometimes, Dylan could be hard work.

But whatever, I guess I was still determined to help him get himself a best(est) friend.

Even if he drove me mad while I was doing it.

The best-friend poem

So how *could* I help Dylan get some friends?

Well, I couldn't do anything to help right now, because I was in class. It was Friday, and the last day before we broke up for a week's holiday. Our teacher, Miss Levy, looked tired, as if she was really looking forward to the holiday. Or maybe she was just tired of hearing our rubbish poems.

Like the rubbish poem Georgia Jones was reading out right now...

"It's called **Sausages**. It goes,

> My favourite food is
> **SAUSAGES,**
> 'cause they are VERY nice.
> My mum gives me chips with them
> or maybe sometimes rice.

Only I don't really have rice, Miss Levy – I just needed rice to rhyme!"

"Thank you, Georgia, that was very ... *interesting*," said Miss Levy.

Lying is not really a good thing to do, but Miss Levy was lying when she said that Georgia's poem was interesting. Then again, I guess it would have sounded mean to be honest and say it was a bit boring.

Miss Levy had asked us all to write about things that were important to us, but I think she was regretting it now. That's because so far ...

* 8 boys had written about football,
* 6 girls had written about their cats (and all rhymed 'PURR' with 'FUR'),
* 4 boys had written about their Playstation 2 or Xbox and
* 3 girls had written about shopping.

Apart from being about lots of the same things (and sausages), none of the poems was very funny or sad or clever, which is what poems are supposed to be, I guess.

At least my best(est) friends had *tried* to do something different. Fee's was about her hair (Miss Levy said it was very "positive"), and Soph's was about her dance class ("I like the rhythm of it," said Miss Levy, "but it *is* on the short side, Sophie!").

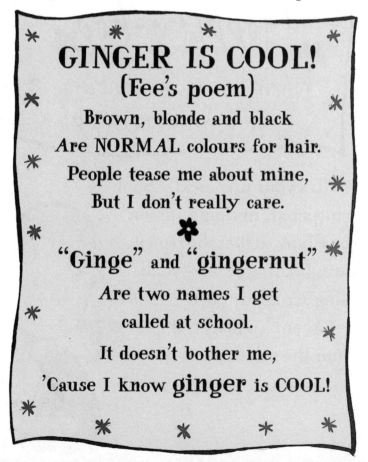

GINGER IS COOL!
(Fee's poem)

Brown, blonde and black
Are NORMAL colours for hair.
People tease me about mine,
But I don't really care.

❋

"Ginge" and "gingernut"
Are two names I get
called at school.
It doesn't bother me,
'Cause I know ginger is COOL!

I LOVE TO DANCE
(Soph's poem)

Skip Hop
Hoppity-hop
When I'm Irish-dancing
I don't want to stop!

"It's your turn next!" Soph whispered, nudging me on the elbow so that the pencil I was holding went skedaddling across my poem.

"Yeah!" whispered Fee from the other side of me.

"And your cat poem is *much* better than any of the others."

I don't mean to sound like a big-headed, *I'M-SO-FAB* show-off, but my cat poem *was* better than the others. For a start, I hadn't used the words 'PURR' or 'FUR', never mind rhymed them. And instead of just going on and on about how cute my cat was (like everyone else had done), I'd written about how hard it was to tell the difference between Smudge and a cushion, but that I *still* loved her.

"Er… I'm not going to read that one out," I mumbled, turning my scrawled-on page over to a newer, neatly-written-on page.

"Are you feeling shy 'cause you're last to stand up and read?" Fee whispered some more.

"Or is it 'cause all the other cat poems are rotten and you don't want to show them up?" asked Soph, *forgetting* to whisper.

For that, Soph got a wide-eyed, warning look from Miss Levy, while I got dirty looks from the six girls who'd written about their moggies.

"Come on then, Indie!" Miss Levy said directly to me. "Let's hear what's important to *you*!"

"OK," I said in a small nervous squeak, kind of 'cause I still felt bad for the cat fans, and kind of 'cause *everyone* was looking at me.

For a second I wished I was a pupil at Harry Potter's school and could magic myself invisible so everyone would stop staring. But I didn't go to Hogwarts; I went to West Green Primary School for ordinary, non-magical children and I just *had* to get on with it, since everyone else had done it already.

"It's called

A BEST FRIEND,"

I began, in as brave a voice as I could manage (which probably sounded as brave as a kitten mewing).

mew!

"Sounds good!" Miss Levy smiled encouragingly, probably very relieved that my poem wasn't about football, shopping or Playstations.

"Right. It goes like this…"

"Indie, that was lovely! Thank you!" said Miss Levy, beaming at me.

I had no idea if the rest of the class thought my poem was lovely or what, 'cause the end-of-school bell chose that second to go * * *

Briiiiinnnnnnnnnggggggg…!

* and the whole classroom turned into a * blur of girls and boys rushing out to start their holiday straight away.

"See you in a week's time!" I heard Miss Levy call out above the screeching of chairs and yakking of kids.

Meanwhile, I felt a hand slip under each elbow.

"How come you ended up writing a different poem?" asked Fee, thinking back to our scribbles yesterday, before we

got distracted by the gerbil explosion.

"Whatever," shrugged Soph, before I got a chance to answer Fee's question. "But that stuff about not having a best friend ... well, you'll *always* have us, Indie!"

I was confused for a second, till it dawned on me that Soph thought the poem was about *her* and *Fee*.

"But I didn't mean… I mean, it's not about *you* two – it's about Dylan!"

Soph and Fee looked kind of hurt when I said that.

"I wrote it last night," I tried to explain, "after Dylan told me he didn't have any *proper* friends!"

"Oh, that's a shame!" said Fee, with a frown. "WOW – it's really sweet of you to write a poem about him."

"Yeah…" Soph agreed. "Well, I know you feel sorry for Dylan, but don't forget, Indie, me and Fee are your bestest friends in the whole wide world!"

"Dylan says 'bestest' isn't a proper word," I mumbled, remembering what he'd told me yesterday.

"Well, it *isn't*, but we just say it 'cause it's our own, special made-up word, don't we?"

That was Fee, looking a bit hurt.

Again.

"Never mind about swot-boy Dylan," said Soph, sounding kind of annoyed. "Us three are bestest friends – cross our hearts and hope to die!"

"Cross my heart and hope to die!" I repeated, same as the other two.

Though my head was too full of Dylan for me to remember to *actually* cross my heart.

Which is maybe why everything went

wibbly

WOBBLY

and weird

between me and my best(est) friends by the end of the week…

The Very IMPORTANT Project

Me, Soph and Fee usually spent Saturday mornings round one another's houses, watching cartoons, bands and silly stuff on TV.

This morning, it was Fee's turn, so she'd have piled all the cushions from the sofa and chairs on the floor, ready for us all (and her cat Garfield) to splodge out on.

But this particular morning, I wouldn't be doing any splodging. This particular morning, I'd phoned Fee and said I couldn't come.

"Why not?"

"'Cause," I told her, "I have to meet a **VIP**!"

"A **Very Important Person**? Like someone dead famous you mean?"

I could imagine Fee's arched, gingery eyebrows frowning as she spoke. I realized I'd made it sound *way* too exciting and mysterious — she probably thought Madonna was coming round to our house to pick out a couple of gerbils to take home with her as pets.

"No – I mean, a **Very Important Project**!"

That's what I'd decided when I'd been lying in bed last night – everyone needs something interesting to do during the holidays, and I'd made up my mind that making Dylan more friend-friendly would be my **Very Important Project** for the week. I had absolutely no idea how I could do that, but I reckoned I'd have till Sunday – when I went over (as usual) to visit my dad, my step-mum Fiona and Dylan – to work something out.

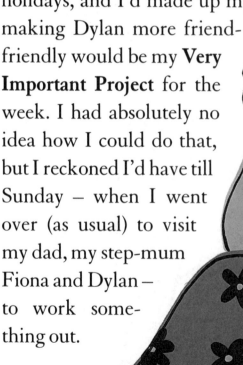

And then Dylan had changed my plans by phoning me first thing this morning.

OK, he didn't so much phone me as photo-message me.

Caitlin our lodger – who looks after me when Mum's working – had just made us both singed sausages and burnt beans for breakfast when I heard my mobile go

PING!

And there on the display was a picture of Dylan in his room, holding up a piece of paper that read,

HELP!
I'm bored!

Well, of *course* he was bored – he didn't have a best friend to hang out with during the holidays.

So I texted him back, asking if he wanted to come round and help me walk the dogs in the park.

He wrote back and said, **Don't u mean they'll walk US in the park?!,** which was pretty funny, *and* true.

So half an hour later, instead of eating cheese on toast on Fee's cushions, I was in the park with Dibbles (dopey dog), George (skinny dog), Kenneth (dog that thinks it's a cat) and Dylan (human – I *think*).

"She was a bit freaked."

"Who was a bit freaked about *what*?"

Honestly, having a conversation with Dylan was seriously complicated. It was like being in a maze heading for the middle and then finding yourself on a path taking you back to the beginning again.

No wonder he didn't have a zillion people fighting to be his best friend. And it wasn't *just* the fact that he could be hard work to chat to, it was also the clothes he wore. I mean, those *terrible* red trousers he had on, and that yellow T-shirt with the teddy bear

logo on it… I know Dylan is kind of small for his age, but there's no excuse for dressing like a five-year-old.

'Course I knew who was choosing his clothes for him: Fiona. And much as I liked my step-mum, I didn't like the way she tried to wrap Dylan up in a *mountain* of cotton wool, as if the bogey man or every germ in the world would get him if she didn't look out for him every second of the day.

"My mum," Dylan interrupted my thoughts, "She was pretty freaked out about me coming to the park on my own today."

I might have known.

"But you're *not* on your own!" I blurted out. "You're with me, and three dogs, and about ... about fifty other people!"

The fifty other people included parents cooing over wailing, dribbly babies in pushchairs, parents shouting at toddlers who were hitting other toddlers, bunches of girls sitting chatting on benches, and groups of boys or older blokes enthusiastically playing games of football.

"Yeah, that's what

Mike – I mean your dad – told her," said Dylan, picking up a stick and chucking it so the dogs could chase it (George and Kenneth bolted after it, but Dibbles was too dense to notice and went to sniff an empty crisp packet instead.)

Poor Dylan.

Y'know, it's every mum's job to worry, but Fiona really was an expert worrier – as well as being an expert tidier and an expert cook.

My mum, on the other hand, was pretty and sweet and ditzy and forgetful and smelled of hamster bedding a lot of the time. And when I say forgetful, I mean she sometimes forgot stuff like mealtimes 'cause she was so caught up in the animals she looked after. But me and our lodger Caitlin and the microwave managed fine, if she was in one of her disorganized moods. And Mum was maybe forgetful, but she always looked out for me and taught me the important stuff like being safe. In fact, she'd once scribbled me a **Safe Stuff** list and it was pinned to the fridge (and to the inside of my brain).

It said …

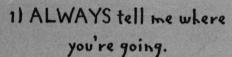

1) ALWAYS tell me where you're going.

2) Phone me if you're going to be later back than you thought.

3) Go places with your friends, or take the dogs with you.

4) Be NICE and POLITE to people, but don't go near cars or houses of strangers or people you don't know very well.

5) Have FUN ... but out of the corner of your eye, watch out for **weirdos.**

I was just about to tell Dylan about the **Safe Stuff** list when—

"So how can I get friends?"

He was off again, darting in a different direction (as usual).

"Well ..." I said thoughtfully (trying to hide the fact that I hadn't worked out a proper plan to help him yet), "... if you could choose, what *would* your best friend be like?"

"Like one of them," said Dylan, pointing shyly ahead.

I looked past the three dogs in front of us (two of them twirling round in a pointlessly happy way, and one poo-ing) and realized that Dylan was pointing at some lads kicking a football around.

The lads looked about nine or ten, and had on football shirts and cool, long-ish sk8tr-boi shorts. As they ran around, calling out to each other in a chilled-out way, you could tell they probably all had favourite bands and favourite football players and favourite styles of skateboard.

 Meanwhile, Dylan probably had a favourite fossil, a favourite type of sum and a favourite pair of Spider-Man pyjamas.

And there wasn't anything wrong with fossils and sums and Spider-Man pyjamas … unless you wanted to fit in with boys as cool as that lot.

"That's Matt and Zane and Rez and some other guys from my school!" said Dylan enthusiastically. "They don't really talk to me, but I'd really, *really* like to be friends with them!"

Uh-oh.

My **Very Important Project** was looking **VHA**, which stands for **Very Hard, Actually**…

What NOT to wear

How to make Dylan more friend-friendly – well, the first thing we had to sort out was clothes. Those cool boys in the park weren't going to think his T-shirt with the teddy-bear logo on it was cool, *that* was for sure…

"So, what do you fancy doing this afternoon?" Dad asked me and Dylan, as he and Fiona tidied up and filled the dishwasher.

It was Sunday. I always spent the day at my dad's house on Sunday. Being mega-neat and pet-free, Dad's place wasn't as much fun as Mum's. Then again, my dad and Fiona *did* have an ace collection of DVDs, and if we didn't end up going out together somewhere on Sunday afternoon, then we'd stay in and watch one of those. (I did once suggest taking all the cushions off the sofa and chairs like Fee does on Saturday mornings, but Fiona looked a bit ill

and so I shut up about it.)

"Me and Dylan have got stuff to do," I answered Dad's question, sticking my thumb over in Dylan's direction.

Dad and Fiona looked chuffed and confused at the same time. I guess they were confused because for years, me and Dylan got on OK-ish, but weren't exactly big buddies. And I guess they were chuffed because it finally looked like we were getting along pretty well.

Actually, we'd been getting along pretty good since Dylan helped me try to find a home for Dibbles. Dibbles had been bypassed by new owners at the *Paws For Thought* Animal Rescue Centre due to the fact that he wasn't very cute and had a special blankie that smelt like a swamp. Me and Dylan worked very hard at giving Dibbles a new image, and that's *exactly* what I was going to do for Dylan now.

"What stuff have you two got to do, then?" Dad asked, as he put the last fork in the dishwasher.

"Computer stuff," I shrugged.

I didn't want to say out loud that I was checking out Dylan's wardrobe for anything with teddies and sailboats on it, in case I offended Fiona, since I was pretty sure *she* was the one who bought that kind of thing.

"What computer stuff?" Dylan asked, wondering what I was on about.

"Just the *stuff*!" I said vaguely, widening my eyes at my step-brother to show that we were talking in secret code.

Dylan might be very good at tests and exams, but he obviously wasn't very good at talking in secret code – probably because he'd never had a proper best friend to talk in secret code *with*.

I could tell from his puzzled expression that he was *just* about to say,"*What* stuff?", so I bundled Dylan towards his bedroom before he got any further than, "*Wha*—?".

"Look," I said, as I sat down on his whirly desk chair, "I made the excuse about the computer because we're going to figure out what clothes you've got that look kind of cool, and which are pants. And I didn't want to hurt your mum's feelings, since she buys your clothes for you."

"Oh, OK," nodded Dylan, now that he understood.

Almost.

"Er, Indie…"

"What?" I said, as I started to rummage through a random drawer.

"Why?"

"Why what?" I asked him right back.

"*Why* are we figuring out which clothes are **cool** and which are **pants?**"

cool

pants

"Because if you want to be friends with those boys in the park, then you have to dress like them, and not like their kid brother," I explained, holding up a baseball cap with a toy digger on it as an example.

Dylan was an excellent pupil. He sat patiently on the end of his bed and listened very, very hard while I went through his wardrobe and drawers and pointed out what was fine and what was horrible.

In the end, I'd rearranged his stuff around so it would be easy for him to figure out what not to wear – I'd made an 'urgh' drawer.

The 'urgh' drawer contained:

🙁 *anything* with teddies on it,

🙁 some shorts in pastel stripes,

🙁 a jumper with a cuddly bunny sewn on

the front,

🙁 a T-shirt with the slogan 'Mummy's Little Rascal!' and

🙁 a pair of musical socks that played

Happy Birthday!

"So, what must you *never* do from now on?" I asked Dylan, in my most teacherly voice.

"Wear anything from the 'urgh' drawer," Dylan recited, like the good pupil he was.

"*And?*"

"And when I go out shopping with my mum, I mustn't let her buy me anything that looks like anything from the 'urgh' drawer."

♩ ♩ ♫ ♪

I suddenly felt very proud of Dylan,
just like his (real) teacher at school must've
done every time he scored mega-good
marks for something.

I felt even *more* proud half an hour
later, when Dad shouted that it was time to
give me a lift home, and me and the new,
improved Dylan
walked into
the living room.

"Hey, *you're*
looking very
trendy, young
man!" Dad
grinned at the
sight of Dylan.
"Is that my
baseball
cap?"

Dylan *was* looking quite trendy (in a plain black T-shirt and jeans), and it *was* Dad's baseball cap (a nicely faded blue one, instead of the toy digger).

Fiona wasn't so keen, even if she didn't say so. In the car over to my place, she kept turning around and checking Dylan out. She almost seemed sad that Dylan looked like a proper nine-year-old boy instead of a toddler.

"What are you up to tomorrow, Indie? Seeing the girls?" asked Dad, as we turned into my road.

"Mmm…" I nodded in reply, sneaking a sideways peek at Dylan and thinking he didn't look enough like the boys from his class yet. What was it that made him look different? I frowned, trying to put my finger on it…

"Hey, Dylan, don't forget it's my day off tomorrow," said Dad, pulling up outside my house. "So are we on for going to the barber's together?"

An idea suddenly *boinged* into my head faster than Dylan could say yes.

"Can I come?" I blurted out, now that I'd realized that the *one* thing that made Dylan different from the boys in his class was his haircut. I mean, it was fine, it was

OK, but he didn't look as cool as those lads.

"Yeah, can Indie come?" Dylan jumped in too.

Dad and Fiona exchanged the smallest, weeniest surprised glance, but I saw it. They obviously thought it meant me and Dylan were getting to be *really* good friends.

What they *didn't* realize was that it was just all part of my **Very Important Project**. We had one week before Dylan went back to school, and I wanted to make him a *lot* more friend-friendly by then.

And tomorrow, I was going to make sure that his *hair* was friend-friendly too!

I was feeling very pleased with myself as I stood on the pavement, ready to wave Dad, Fiona and Dylan off.

That was till I noticed something very,

very bad.

In fact, it was something

very,

very

urgh

indeed…!

!

The cooler than cool hedgehog haircut

"Why is **I ❤ MUM** 'urgh'?" said Dylan, without looking up from the magazine he was reading.

It might have sounded like the beginning of a riddle, but Dylan was just asking why his **I ❤ MUM** socks had to go and live in the 'urgh' drawer for ever.

I'd spotted the **I ❤ MUM** socks yesterday afternoon. Dylan had put his foot up

on the back seat and pulled one of them up, just as Dad's car pulled away from the pavement.

I hadn't been able to say anything about it yesterday (since cars go a lot faster than my legs do, and I wouldn't have been able to catch them up). But now that we were in the barber's – and Dad was just out of listening range – I'd explained to Dylan why the socks had to go.

Or at least I *thought* I had.

"Dylan, **I ❤ MUM** isn't '**urgh**' –
I ❤ MUM is cute! But not on socks when
you're a nine-year-old boy!"

Especially not when you were a nine-year-old boy who wanted to hang out
with the cool lads in your class.

"But that's not fair!" Dylan
mumphed, still not looking up
from his magazine.

"*What's* not fair?" (Why
doesn't Dylan ever ask a
proper, whole question that
you can understand, instead of
you having to ask another
question first? That boy *really*
makes my head go dizzy sometimes…)

"*Soph's* got a T-shirt with
I ❤ Kittens on it!"

"Yes, but girls can *always* wear cute stuff, however old they are. Boys can only do cute stuff till they're five or six."

Dylan made a little noise that might have been a huffy sort of "huh!", but I couldn't hear him properly. The barber shop was very noisy – nearly as noisy as the *Paws For Thought* Animal Rescue Centre when Mum's doing the rounds with the breakfast munchies.

But instead of happy woofs, howls and miaows this was a different type of noisy.

For a start, there was a TV in the corner babbling, then there was a fan on the ceiling whoosh-whooshing, plus lots of razors buzz-buzzing, AND plenty of men and boys chatting at the level of a YELL above all the babbling, whooshing and buzzing.

Bzzz

Dad was sitting on a seat up at the far end of the barber's, with his nose in a photography magazine, while one of the barber blokes buzzed around his head with a razor.

One of the other barbers had led Dylan to a tall, black vinyl seat in front of a mirror, but hadn't started cutting yet – which was good, since I needed to show him the picture I had in my pocket first…

"What are you reading anyway?" I asked Dylan, as I perched my bum on the empty black vinyl seat just along from him.

Dylan answered my reflection in the mirror, instead of the *real* me.

"A thing about the latest operating system for my computer," he replied, holding up his magazine so I could see the cover.

But because I was staring at it in the mirror, it was back-to-front and kind of hard to read.

"**SULP CP**…"

I muttered, narrowing my eyes.

So … Dylan was reading about the latest operating systems in a magazine called **SULP CP**. For all that meant to me, he might as well have been speaking in a very complicated language like Russian or something.

"**PC PLUS**," he corrected me.

"Oh," I mumbled, wriggling in my chair and feeling dumb.

I thought for a second about asking

him what an 'operating system' was, but I knew I wouldn't understand the answer.

"So what's it like?"

Sigh. That was Dylan, saying something *else* I didn't understand.

"What's *what* like?" I frowned at him.

"My new haircut!"

OK – now I got him. I hopped off the slithery black chair and fished the photo out of the pocket

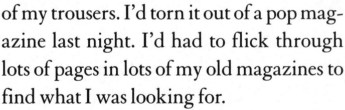

of my trousers. I'd torn it out of a pop magazine last night. I'd had to flick through lots of pages in lots of my old magazines to find what I was looking for.

"He looks like a hedgehog," mumbled Dylan, staring at the head of the grinning guy in the photo.

"He does *not* look like a hedgehog! He looks cool!" I said, defending the boy in the boy band with the spiky hair. "He looks just like those lads you pointed out in the park! What are their names again?"

"Matt and Zane and Rez."

"Well, if you want to fit in with Matt and Zane and Rez, you have to look like them and have a haircut like theirs."

"I guess…" said Dylan warily, obviously still thinking of spike-a-delic hedgehogs.

And then I realized something; I didn't know why exactly Dylan wanted to be friends with those particular boys.

"What's so great about Matt and Zane and Rez anyway? You said they didn't even talk to you!"

"They don't," Dylan replied, blinking

his blue eyes at me. "But they're always talking to each other, and it always looks like they're having a laugh. Like you and Soph and Fee."

I felt a funny **ping** when he said their names. What did that **ping** mean? Never mind; I had more important things to figure out, like how to convince Dylan that he wouldn't end up looking like a hedgehog.

And persuading the barber bloke to cut it like that. ("Are you sure? Maybe I'd better check with his father first…")

And persuading Dad that it would be absolutely and totally cruel not to let Dylan have that haircut. ("Dad, every boy in his class has one just like it! He'd be the odd one out!")

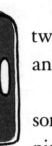

It was me against two men and a boy — and I won.

Ten minutes and some buzzing and snipping later, Dylan had a very cool, very spiky hairdo.

"WOW!" said Dylan, gazing at himself in the mirror.

"Hmm," muttered the barber with one eyebrow raised.

"Well, it's very … *interesting!*" mumbled Dad, sounding like Miss Levy (lying).

* * *eek!* * gasped someone from the barber shop doorway.

And that someone happened to be

Fiona, looking as shocked as if she'd been zapped by a stray bolt of lightning.

But as lightning doesn't usually happen inside shops, I guessed that she wasn't very pleased to see Dylan's new friend-friendly look.

Still, that was a good sign. If *Fiona* hated it, then Matt, Zane and Rez would probably think it was cooler than cool!

And sooner rather than later, me and Dylan would need to test that out…

eek!

Dylan gets the wobbles

"I was trying to stroke the babies but I think the mum gerbil thought I was going to hurt them, so she bit me. See?"

I held up my finger to show Dylan my wound from this morning (OK, a couple of tiny teeth-marks that were practically invisible to the human eye).

It was Tuesday and we were in

the park again. George, Kenneth and Dibbles were very happy that

a) it was the school holidays, and

b) I was doing a **Very Important Project,** mainly because it meant extra walkies for *them.*

Speaking of walkies, Dylan stopped strolling and stared closely at my finger. From here I got a close-up of his very cool spiky hair. He'd had it for 24 hours now, and it still looked good. It *hadn't* gone freaky and weird while he was sleeping (like mine always did) and Fiona *hadn't* dragged him back to the barber's to trade the spikes for something more sensible (which I was scared she'd do).

Dylan blinked his blue eyes at my "wound".

"It bit *really* hard and wouldn't let go," I chattered on. "I had to wander round the house with it dangling from my finger."

"So how did you get it off in the end?"

"Mum knew where to tickle it, and it just opened its mouth to giggle or something and dropped into her hand!"

Knowing how to tickle a grumpy gerbil … it's things like that that make my mum so ace with animals. (Caitlin had just screamed and suggested hitting it with a rolled-up newspaper.)

"I've got a new mouse," Dylan suddenly announced, as he stood up straight and carried on walking.

OK, so I could forgive Dylan for changing the subject – as usual. But if Fiona had suddenly gone and let him have a pet, how could he have bought a mouse, when he knew that the *Paws For Thought* Animal Rescue Centre (and our kitchen) was bursting at the seams with gerbils in need of a good home?

"Where did you get it?" I asked him, ready to thump him if he said a pet shop and not a rescue centre like Mum's.

"The electrical shop in the high street."

"What?!" I said, completely confused. "But that sells stuff like phones and cameras and everything!"

"Yeah, *so*?"

"So when did they start selling *mice*?"

"They've *always* sold computer stuff."

Duh… Dylan was talking about a plastic computer mouse, and not a sweet'n'squeaky live mouse. He really was the most annoying boy to have a conversation with.

Luckily, I wasn't going to be having a conversation with him for too much longer – Matt, Zane and Rez were.

"Look, Dyl! Your mates are playing football over there again!"

"Well, they're not my mates—"

"*Yet*!" I jumped in, trying to be extra-positive. "So why don't you walk over and say hi?!"

Dylan suddenly looked very sheepish, which is fine if you're a sheep but not so good if you're a boy.

"It would look weird if I just walked over…"

Dylan wasn't getting out of it now. He was dressed right and had the right hair to fit in with those boys. Now was the perfect time to practise his friend-friendliness.

"It won't look weird if you've got a dog with you!" I told him, quickly clipping a lead on George and handing it to him.

I'd chosen George because he was the coolest-looking of my three dogs. Let's face it, a small Scottish Highland terrier that thought it was a cat *wasn't* too cool (specially when he sometimes broke into howls that sound like **miaows**). And Dibbles … well, Dibbles was adorable but did look like a stuffed bin bag on legs (and if an ice-cream van started playing a tune anywhere near the park, he'd probably end up dragging Dylan under a bench to hide).

Yep, George the tall, sporty-looking greyhound was definitely the best choice.

"Do I have to?" Dylan asked me, eyes pleading.

I knew he was getting the wobbles (and butterflies seemed to be trampolining in my tummy too), but he had to start somewhere. And he was starting with a hi, which wasn't too hard.

"Go on – I'll watch you from behind this tree!"

Very,
very,
verrrrryyyy
sllllloooow
wwwwlllly,

Dylan turned and started heading towards the boys playing football.

"Come on, Dylan!" I whispered, as I peeked out from the side of the big oak tree.

"Hunummmmph, hunummmphhh..."

humphed Dibbles, as he settled himself on one of my feet and lifted his back leg to scratch his ear (not as easy as it sounds, as Dibbles is very round and blobby and his leg is short and doesn't quite reach).

Well, Dibbles didn't seem to mind waiting while Dylan and George walked in slow motion towards the lads, but *Kenneth* was pretty annoyed.

Meee-howwwwwwwww!

he howled up at me grumpily, wondering why we weren't getting on with our walk.

"Shush, Kenneth!" I told him, hoping none of Dylan's maybe new friends were looking over. It would seem pretty strange to see a girl peeking out from a behind a tree, with one loudly miaowing dog and another one that was sitting cross-eyed, frantically scratching at thin air with its back leg.

I picked up a stick ad threw it, hoping that would keep Kenneth happy for a bit. As I did that, I kept my eyes firmly glued to Dylan. He was right beside the boys now … he was lifting his hand to say hi … what would happen nex—

Diddly-iddly-ooo!!

Good grief, a text message. I rummaged in my pocket and checked out my phone.

Wot u up 2? Soph xx

With Dylan, I speedily texted back. **Can't talk – spk l8r. Indie x**

I'd just typed that quick kiss in when a damp grey nose started sniffing at my phone, just in case it turned out to be some new-fangled type of bone or something.

"You're back quick!" I said to Dylan, while scratching George on the head. "What happened?"

"I said hi, like you told me to."

"And then what?"

"And then Rez said hi back, and the other two nodded."

"And then what?"

"And then I didn't know what to say 'cause you hadn't told me anything else, so I just turned round and came back."

Good grief. Had that barber shaved a bit of brain out of Dylan's head yesterday? He might be a bit of a genius, but he could also be *such* a doughball.

As for the **Very Important Project**, it looked like I needed to set Dylan a *lot* more home-work…

Hello, and, er ... goodbye!

It was quarter to three on Wednesday afternoon, and it was raining cats and dogs.

Which is a *very* stupid expression, 'cause I've never seen a raindrop that reminded me much of a cat or a dog. A baby slug, *maybe*. ("It's raining baby slugs!" Yeah, that was definitely better!)

"Er ... did I already give you a tray with juice and biscuits on it?" Mum asked, standing in the doorway of the living room with a gerbil on her shoulder and a tin of cat food in one hand.

"No, Mrs Kidd," said Fee very politely.

Soph and Fee were very used to Mum being a bit ditzy. Other mums' heads are full of thoughts like "I'll have to get off work early to take my kid to the dentist" and "better get something from the supermarket for tea", but my mum's head is just full of fur and feathers and gerbil bedding.

"Wonder where I put it down then...?" she muttered wandering off down the hall.

It was officially a day off for her (and a day off for Caitlin minding me) but then Mum never *really* has a day off when there are fostered animals at home to feed and fuss over.

"So, do you fancy it, then, Indie?" Soph suddenly asked me.

"Fancy what?" I said, checking the

clock on the
mantelpiece
again.

It was nearly ten
to three. Dylan had *exactly*
twelve minutes to get back
to me with the homework
I'd set him. When it had
started raining this morning
and we realized we couldn't go to
the park again, I suggested he sat
down and wrote down five
things he could've said to Matt, Zane and
Rez after he'd said hi to them yesterday.

So, I'd given Dylan till three o'clock to
do it, but knowing what a swotty smart
kid he was, I thought he'd write back in
ten minutes. But I was still waiting, which
meant he was finding it hard. Harder than

maths and science and all that hard stuff put together.

"Do you fancy going to the skating rink with us tomorrow afternoon?" said Soph, sort of almost *scowling* at me.

 Maybe she was almost sort of scowling at me because she'd said that already (it sounded familiar…).

"Um, no I can't. I said I'd see Dylan. If it's nice, we're going to go to the park again, so he can practise saying new things to the lads from his class. But I don't know why he wants to be their friend so much 'cause they never talk to him or anything so they can't be very nice or—"

Brrrr-brrrp! Brrrr-brrrp! Brrrr-brrrp!

At the sound of the phone (and Kenneth mee-howling, and the clatter of the kitchen bin as Dibbles ran to hide from the noise) I didn't get my sentence finished.

"Got to get this!" I said, hurtling towards the phone.

"I only got to three."

That was Dylan. Of course. And of course you always know when it's Dylan because he never bothers with "hello" and

"how're you?" like normal people.

"OK, so what's the three?" I asked, settling myself sideways on a slither of the chair nearest the phone, since Smudge was taking up most of the rest of the space.

"Well, number one is—"

"Oh, hold on a sec, Dylan!" I interrupted as I felt someone tapping at my arm.

It was Fee waving at me and mouthing "see you later". Soph was already at the living-room door. She wasn't waving and she wasn't mouthing "bye" or whatever.

How weird that they were leaving so soon. They'd only turned up out of the blue twenty minutes ago, and they hadn't even had their juice and biscuits yet.

"Bye then!"

"Who are you saying bye to?" Dylan

asked.

"Soph and Fee," I answered, as I gently squidged Smudge over a bit and heard the front door go clunk. "So what's number one on your list, then?"

"My number one is—"

"Oh, hold on a sec, Dylan!" I interrupted again.

Mum had just walked in the living room with the tray (at last). The gerbil wasn't in sight, but there *was* a BIG tin-of-cat-food shape in the pocket of her green, baggy trousers. I really hoped she hadn't accidentally put the gerbil in her *other* pocket...

"Where've Soph and Fee gone?" she asked, looking surprised.

"They just left," I told her.

"Already?" said Mum with a frown.

And when she frowned like that, something went **ping** in my chest again, just like it had a couple of days ago.

Oh no, was I suffering from some terrible condition? ("I'm sorry, Mrs Kidd … your daughter's got a serious attack of the **pings!**")

I'd better be all right – I only had four days of the **Very Important Project** left, and I couldn't go dying of pings before I found Dylan a proper friend!

Secret spying

Here were Dylan's Top Three Things To Say After 'Hi':

1) I've had a haircut.
2) This dog is called George.
3) I'd like a new operating system for my computer.

"I can't believe it took you all day yesterday to come up with this!" I told Dylan, as I looked at the neatly printed (but very empty) A4 sheet in my hand.

We were in the park again. Hiding behind a bush to be exact. It was quite a big bush, 'cause it had to hide me, Dylan, George, Kenneth and Dibbles. We were watching Matt and Zane and Rez playing football again. It was a little bit uncomfortable 'cause after all the rain yesterday, the chunk of park we were standing on was kind of muddy, and some of the mud had found a hole in my trainer to seep through.

"What's wrong with my **'Things To**

Say' list?" Dylan asked, but you could tell by his face he knew they were rubbish.

"Dylan, you can't just say 'Hi' to someone, and then they say 'Hi' and you blurt out 'This dog is called George' or whatever."

"Can't you?"

"No! At the beginning of a conversation, you have to say stuff like 'What're you up to?' And then they'd say 'Playing football. What're *you* up to?' And then you could say you're walking your friend's dog. Matt and that lot might say he's cool, and you could say 'Yes he is, and his name's George'. See?"

Dylan blinked hard at me.

"All that takes a long time. Why can't I just tell them his name's George straight away?"

"'Cause it's too weird!" I blurted out, suddenly realizing that the way my super-smart step-brother thought and spoke was maybe what was *really* putting people off being friends with him, *more* than the I ♥ MUM socks.

And maybe saying it was *weird* was too harsh (even if it was true). Maybe I could put it another way.

"Look, Dylan, you're good at studying stuff, aren't you?" I said, as I felt one foot get more and more squelchy.

"I guess so," answered Dylan, peering off now at the lads playing their game.

"Well, why don't you study the way people talk to each other?" I suggested. "You could watch and listen to people, and—"

"They're pack- ing up! They're going!" Dylan interrupted me suddenly, pointing at Matt and Zane and Rez.

But I didn't mind being interrupted too much, 'cause it gave me an idea…

"Come on," I said hurriedly, clipping on the leads of the dogs.

"Come on what?" asked Dylan, looking a little bit alarmed.

"We're going to follow those boys and see what they do and where they're going. It might give you ideas about what to speak to them about when you see them next time!"

A smile beamed onto Dylan's face, and off we went, squelching (in secret) after Matt, Zane and Rez…

✳ ✳ ✳

Dibbles didn't like the high street very much.

It wasn't the traffic noise and the bustle that freaked him out, it was sound of the **bleep-bleep-bleep!** green man at all the pedestrian crossings. As soon as he heard a **bleep-bleep-bleep!**, he closed his eyes and tried to bury his head in the back of my knees, which made it kind of hard to walk.

Anyway, we'd walked all the way to the high street following Matt, Zane and Rez. It had been hard to make sure they didn't see us – the five of us had to run into lots of doorways or pretend to be very interested in shop windows (I didn't like it when we had to pretend to be interested in the butcher's shop, but the dogs sniffed like crazy).

So far we had watched the lads laugh and chat as they wandered into a CD shop,

a shop that sold trainers and a newsagent. We hadn't been close enough to hear what they were saying though. But that was all about to change…

"Have you got any money on you?" I asked Dylan, as Matt, Zane and Rez wandered into a packed burger place and joined the queue.

"Not much," he said, pulling a few pence out of his jeans pocket.

I didn't have much either, but Dylan quickly figured out we had enough to buy the smallest bag of chips.

"Right, get in the queue and listen to them!" I ordered Dylan, jerking forward as a green man crossing **bleep-bleep-bleep**-ed somewhere nearby and Dibbles battered into the back of my knees. "And if they notice you, say Hi …

and then something like, 'Can you see how much the chips cost?'"

"But I can see how much the chips cost! It says so on the plastic sign above the counter!"

"Dylan, stop being so logical," I sighed. "I'm trying to find a way for you to get talking to those boys!"

"Ah… OK."

As Dylan finally went in and joined the queue, I hunkered down beside the dogs, scratching all three heads in turn, and wishing I had an extra hand so no one felt left out. And all the time, I kept peeking in at Dylan to see how he was getting on.

He was listening to the boys, I could tell (I just wished he wouldn't keep looking from one to the other as they chatted and making it so obvious, that was all).

And then something brilliant happened... One of the boys (I didn't know which was which) turned to Dylan and

said "Hi". Although I was looking at the back of his head, I was pretty sure Dylan said "Hi" back. Now all I could do was keep my fingers (and toes) crossed and hope he wouldn't blurt out something *weird*-sounding.

Well, he must have said something *normal*-sounding, 'cause next thing, all three boys were talking and grinning with him.

* ☆ Wow! * ☆

It had worked! I'd made Dylan a bit more friend-friendly! Except oops, they all turned round and looked towards the big glass window, and I didn't want Dylan's maybe new friends to see me and blow his cool.

I was still bent down on my haunches talking to the dogs, but that wasn't enough to hide me, so I did a quick sideways waddle, like a cross between a duck and a frog, till I was away from the window and safely out of sight.

George, Kenneth and Dibbles thought this was an excellent game and started licking and swirling around me till I was in a knot of dog drool and leads.

"Indie?" said a voice beside me all of a sudden. "Why were you doing that frog-thing just now?"

I looked up and saw Dylan, holding a small bag of chips. So he had seen me waddling out of view – I hoped the other lads hadn't. That would be *so* embarrassing.

"Er, I was just playing around with the dogs, that's all. So? How did you get on?" I asked, straightening myself to a standing position and helping myself to a chip. "You were properly chatting to them!"

"Yeah!" Dylan nodded, looking very chuffed with himself. "And I didn't say anything dumb, I don't think!"

"So, what were you talking about?"

"They want to know which one!" Dylan said brightly.

Ah, good old Dylan and his weird way of talking.

"They want to know which one *what*?" I laughed.

"Which one of them you fancy!"

Uh-oh.

A chip that was on its way to my mouth ended up stuck in mid-air.

"*WHAT!*" I yelped.

"They saw us following them today and they've seen us hanging around in the park watching them all this week," Dylan babbled on, so happy to have had a conversation with his heroes that he didn't seem to notice me squirming.

"They *have?*" I yelped again, feeling the blood in my veins turn cold as ice-lollies.

"Yeah, and they thought I was trying to talk to them to tell them you had a crush on one of them!"

Y'know, round our town, there are plaques on the wall telling you if famous people lived there or important things happened there once upon a long ago time.

Well, I think there should be a plaque on the wall outside Benny's Burgers saying:

**INDIE KIDD
died of shame
on this spot.**

Embarrassed by the Embarrassing Thing

Will we go 2 park today?

It was Friday morning, and even though I thought I'd die of shame yesterday afternoon outside the burger place, I was still alive. (And still very, very, *very* embarrassed.)

And after all that embarrassment, I wasn't in the mood for the **Very**

Important Project today, which is why I texted Dylan straight back and said

Can't. See u Sunday @ Dad's

But if I wasn't in the mood for the **Very Important Project**, what *was* I in the mood for?

I put on the TV, but there were just programmes with people talking about how to paint a wall and how to hammer a nail and it was *way* too boring to take my mind off the Embarrassing Thing.

I tried to go and talk to Caitlin, but she was too busy practising the didgeridoo to talk to me about how embarrassing yesterday was. (Anyway, I think I'd be

too *embarrassed* to tell her about the Embarrassing Thing.)

I tried to go and stroke the baby gerbils, but the mum gerbil hissed at me in a very scary way for something so small so I didn't bother.

I wished Mum wasn't working today so I could talk to her about it. (Actually, that would be too embarrassing too.)

Then I realized that there *was* someone – OK, *two* someones – that I could talk to, who'd understand exactly how I was feeling and say lots of nice things to make me feel better.

Diddly-iddly-ooo!!

Great! A message! Was that Soph or Fee texting, thinking of me at the *exact* second I was thinking of them?

Nope, it was just a photo message from Dylan.

Actually it was a photo message *of* Dylan.

With his mouth turned down, all exaggerated, like a sad clown's, he was holding a piece of paper in front of him that said,

It would've been quite cute, if I wasn't still annoyed with him for talking to those boys in his class about me yesterday. I didn't find out what he'd said to them when they asked which one of them I fancied because I was too embarrassed. I'd just checked that he'd got his bus pass, shoved him on the first bus that went near my dad's place and then ran home. (Which the dogs LOVED, since dogs don't understand about embarrassment and didn't know *that's* why I was running.)

I flipped away from Dylan's photo message without saving it and pressed the speed dial for Fee's, but it was switched off.

So I speed-dialled Soph's mobile, and got through straight away.

Er, *sort of…*

"Hello?" said a voice that sounded an awful lot like Soph's.

"Soph? It's me, Indie!"

Then this bizarre-o thing happened – the phone went all muffly, but I could *almost* hear girls talking in the background.

Er, what was going on?

And then the person who sounded like Soph started speaking again, only it didn't sound so much like Soph now.

(This was getting *seriously* confusing.)

The person was speaking in this

French accent and was saying, "Pardon" (the way French people say it), "but you 'ave ze wrong number. Au revoir."

Before the French person clicked off, I could swear I heard someone somewhere giggling. And as there was no one in my house giggling, then it had to be coming from the other end of the phone.

Urgh.

That weird **pinging** thing was back, pitter-pattering all over my chest and down into my tummy too.

Y'know, Fee once showed me and

121

Sophie a big word in the dictionary that always made her giggle. It was 'discombobulated', which means muddled up. And right now I felt very, very discombobulated.

I'd speed-dialled Soph for sure, so how could I have got a wrong number?

And if I *hadn't* got a wrong number, then – HELP! – what on earth was going on?

Could someone explain ... *please*?!

Bye-bye gerbils (and friends)

It was Saturday morning and it was Soph's turn to have us all round at her place to watch TV. But she hadn't called last night to say it was definitely on, and she hadn't called this morning either.

And I was still so discom-wotsit after that freaky French phone call yesterday that I hadn't wanted to call *her*.

So when Mum asked if I wanted to come take a drive with her in the big, rattly

Rescue Centre Van that smelt a bit of straw and disinfectant, I'd said yes please thank you very much. 'Specially since my only other choice was to stay home and listen to Caitlin practising on her didgeridoo again, while the dogs joined in with a *howl*-along.

"You're looking a bit sad today, Indie," said Mum, sneaking a sideways peek at me as the van stopped at a set of traffic lights. "Are you sad to see the gerbils go?"

We'd just dropped off our foster gerbils to a lovely lady at an animal sanctuary in the countryside, who said she'd love them and cuddle them (if their mum let her) and find them new homes.

"I'm a bit sad because of that," I told her, my eyes twinkling as I remembered

the babies' noses twitching, testing the smell of country air. "But I'm more sad 'cause I think Soph and Fee have gone funny on me."

"How exactly have they gone funny on you?" asked Mum, pushing her tangly blonde hair away from her face. (There was a tiny gerbil-sized muddy paw-print on her cheek. She must have got that when she was kissing the grumpy mum gerbil bye-bye.)

"It's like they don't want to be friends with me any more."

I'd decided that last night when I'd been lying in bed. That's 'cause I'd been thinking a lot about that 'wrong number'.

I really didn't think it could be a wrong number. And I'd thought of something important – Soph is half-French (her other half's Somali) and she can speak French very, very well…

"Well, you haven't spent much time with them this week, have you, Indie?" said Mum, driving on and fixing her eyes on the road ahead. "You only saw them once, and that's when *they* dropped in to see *you*!"

"But that's not fair!"

I told her, feeling hurt that she seemed to be on Soph and Fee's side. "I've been helping Dylan!"

"I know, and that's really kind of you, but perhaps the girls have felt neglected. After all, the three of you normally see each other *all* the time…"

Actually, I was glad Mum's eyes were fixed on the road ahead – it meant she didn't see that my eyes had gone prickly with tears.

We were both quiet for a minute, which was good 'cause I got the chance to stare out of the window and try and blink my tears back.

"Listen, Indie," said Mum finally, "it's still early – it's not even midday. Why don't you call Soph and Fee and see if they want to meet up? You could take them to the café – I'll give you extra pocket money so you can treat them!"

I really didn't know if I was brave enough to phone. But I really knew I missed Soph and Fee. So, with lots of funny **pings** pinging around in my chest, I speed-dialled Fee (at least *she* wouldn't speak to me in French).

"Hello?" said Fee, with the noise of traffic somewhere behind her.

"Hi, s'me," I said nervously.

There was a tiny pause, like Fee was thinking or something, and then she said, "Who?"

A big, painful **ping** went off in my

chest then – she *knew* it was me and was just being mean.

"It's me – Indie!"

"Oh. Hello."

"Um … are you doing anything just now?"

"Uh … how come?"

"'Cause I thought maybe me and you and Soph could meet up at the café. I'll buy us all ice-cream!"

"Where's Dylan, then?"

"Huh? I … I don't know. So can you come?"

"No," Fee mumbled flatly, "I'm out with my mum. And I think Soph said she was going out with her mum too."

"Oh, OK," I mumbled in return. "See you later, then?"

"Whatever," said Fee and then the phone went dead.

"Not good?" said Mum gently, as we stopped at another set of traffic lights close to home.

"No. I think they *are* annoyed with me," I said sadly, thinking how sarky Fee had sounded when she'd asked where Dylan was. "Fee said she couldn't come 'cause she was out with her mum."

"Well, maybe she is!" said Mum with a shrug. "Never mind, Indie – you'll be back at school on Monday and then I'm sure everything will get back to norm—"

"Mum!" I interrupted her.

"LOOK!"

And she looked. And what she saw was the same as me: Soph and Fee strolling to the shops together, all alone, without any mums.

And that's when I knew that I'd been working so hard on Dylan and the **Very Important Project,** that oops, I'd lost my best(est) friends.

And, oops, now that I'd started to cry, I didn't know if I'd ever stop...

Getting a LOT confused

You could tell that Fiona felt **really** sorry for me. I'd dropped at least six big crumbs on the floor and she hadn't made a little hurt face or tried to casually pick them up or anything.

"Have another piece, Indie," Fiona beamed at me, trying to offer another slice of home made sticky toffee 'n' banana cheesecake.

"I don't think I can," I mumbled,

looking sadly at the gorgeous pudding that I'd normally have had three pieces of (at least). "My chest's too sore with **ping**ing."

"The **ping**ing's just a little bit of stress," said Dad, giving me my hundredth hug of the day so far.

"Can you get **ping**ing when you're guilty too?" I asked him, thinking of the very first **ping** I felt in the park, when I didn't answer Soph's text.

"Yep, I guess a bad

case of guilt *could* set off a **ping** or two," Dad nodded.

It was Sunday and I was over at Dad's as usual. I'd tried to put on something that I hoped looked like a happy face, but as soon as I got through the door and Dad said, "What's up with *you,* pumpkin?" I'd had a bad case of prickles of the eyes and splurged the whole thing out.

I hadn't even been embarrassed when Dylan came and stood at the living-room door and listened for a bit. But then he disappeared and I didn't know if I was glad (so he wouldn't see me all prickly eyed), or if I was bugged (since helping him was the reason I'd lost my bestest friends).

"I'm sure things will work out fine with Sophie, and er, Sophie. Friendships often have their ups and downs, Indie," said Fiona, sounding so warm and kindly that my eyes started prickling extra hard. "But I just want to say thank you for being such a good friend to Dylan!"

So that's why she was trying not to mind the crumbs and being v. v. especially nice. As Dylan's mum, she must've worried about him not having any mates to hang out with in the holidays, and at least I'd tried to *get* him some. *And* hung out with him.

Diddly-iddly-ooo!!

Oh … a text. Maybe it was from Mum, asking me to pick up cat litter later on the way home with Dad or something.

Miss u 2. Sorry. C U later this aft? Soph xxx

"Who's that, then?" asked Dad, leaning over for a nosey.

"It's Soph!" I said, holding the phone over for him to read what she'd written.

"She misses you too. Well, that's fantastic!"

It *was* fantastic, I thought, as Dad squeezed my shoulders. But it was also a bit confusing. Why had she said **Miss U 2'**? I hadn't told her I missed her. Though I did, tons.

Diddly-iddly-ooo!!

"Ooh, another one – who's this from?" Fiona arched her eyebrows.

Got Dylan's email. He is so cute. Sorry 2. Big hugs Fee x

Dad and I read out in unison.

OK, I wasn't just a bit confused, I was a LOT confused.

"*What* email from Dylan?" I frowned at my phone.

"Well, why don't you go through and ask him?" suggested Dad.

And so I did. And found him sitting at his computer looking kind of smiley but worried. And no wonder – he was wearing everything, and I mean *everything* from the 'urgh' drawer. He had on his fluffy bunny T-shirt *and* his pastel stripey shorts *and* his baseball cap with the truck on it, *and* he even had an **I ♥ MUM** sock on one hand!

"What have you done?" I asked him, wandering over to his side.

"This…"

Dylan clicked on his mouse and an email message popped up. It was addressed to Soph. There was another one in his 'sent' box that was for Fee.

"You sent them messages from here last weekend, so I had their email addresses in the system…" he explained.

I thought and thought for a second, then remembered that last Sunday – when we were sorting out cool clothes from 'urgh' clothes – Dylan had asked me to turn around while he put on the grey T-shirt and jeans. So I'd gone on the computer and emailed my friends while he got changed.

Now that I'd worked that out, I

thought I'd better read what he'd sent them. And what he'd sent was...

From: dylan@networld

To: Sophie

Sent: Sunday

Subject: Indie

Hi. This is Dylan. Indie misses you and is VERY sorry and sad not to be friends. She has not seen you much this week 'cause she had to try to help me be cool so I could maybe get a best friend. It took her a long time to try to help me 'cause it was a very difficult job, as you can see...

And underneath his message was a very funny digital photo of Dylan dressed up like he was now, pulling a silly face and waving his I ❤ MUM hand at the camera.

"So you helped me get my bestest friends back?"

"Well, yeah," Dylan shrugged. "Only there's no such word as 'best—'"

Before Dylan got a chance to correct me, I pulled the peak of his baseball cap down so that all I could see of his face was a big, dopey smile.

My step-brother Dylan … he could be confusing and annoying and make your
head
go
twisty,
but he was dead smart, and like Fee said, he could be quite cute.

"Want to come out with me and Soph and Fee later?" I asked.

"Uh-huh," said Dylan, nodding the peak of his cap.

"Well there's one condition – this lot has got to go back in the 'urgh' drawer!"

"OK," said the I ♥ MUM sock puppet on his hand…

One, two, three best(est) friends!

"Ouch!"

Dylan had just been hit on the head by a frisbee, then fallen backwards over George and Kenneth, who were both better at catching frisbees than Dylan.

"Are you OK?"

asked Soph, looking worried, since she was the one who'd just chucked the frisbee.

"Yeah... I just feel a bit..."

"Discombobulated?" I shouted out with a grin.

"That means 'muddled up'," Fee explained to Dylan, budging up on the park bench so he could sit down between me and her.

"I know," said Dylan, rubbing the bump on his forehead.

"You do?"

Fee's eyes were wide. She loved big words, and seemed very impressed that Dylan knew what such a big word as dis-combobulated meant.

"Sorry, Dyl! But you *are* getting quite good!" Soph called out, as she tried to wrestle the frisbee out of George's mouth.

"Fee, come and play with me till Dylan feels better…!"

It was late afternoon on Sunday and the seven of us were in the park – me, Dylan, Soph, Fee and the dogs.

As Fee went off to frisbee, I passed Dylan my 99 cone, hoping that licking a bit of ice-cream might make up for the bump on his head.

Not that Dylan seemed to *mind* the bump on his head – he was grinning like mad.

"What's up with

you?" I asked him with a frown, worried that he had got that serious bump-on-the-head thing (concussion, I think it's called).

"Nothing! I'm just having fun!"

"You think getting a bump on the head is *fun*?"

He *definitely* had concussion – he wasn't thinking straight.

"Thanks, Indie!" Dylan suddenly turned to me and said, changing the subject, as ever.

"Thanks for what? For a lick of my ice-cream?" I replied, budging over now that Dibbles had humphed himself onto the bench between us and happily started

thudda-dudda-dudding

" his stubby black tail on the wooden bench.

"No – thanks for getting me some best friends!"

"But I didn't *really*," I told Dylan, thinking that he'd only had one, small (embarrassing for me) conversation with Matt, Zane and Rez in the burger bar. That didn't make them best friends exactly, did it?

"Yes, you did get me best friends!" said Dylan, flashing a big, dopey grin my way and handing me my cone back. "You and Soph and Fee are like my best friends now. Aren't you?"

Were we?

Well, I guess I *had* had a lot of fun hanging out with Dylan this week, so yeah, I guess he was my friend. OK, one of my *best* friends. But what about Soph and Fee? They didn't know him all that well, not well enough to call him a best friend, I didn't think.

"Oi! You guys!" Soph yelled over. "Fancy two against two? Dylan can be on my side!"

"No, he won't!" said Fee. "He'll be on *my* side!"

Well, maybe it looked like Soph and Fee were happy to be best friends with Dylan after all!

"Come on, let's play!" I said to Dylan, as I gave the last of my ice-cream cone to Dibbles. (And got a **thudda-dudda-dudda** tail thump thanks.)

"I didn't tell them."

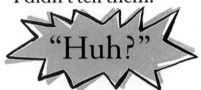

"Huh?"

Dylan, Dylan, Dylan. I didn't think I'd ever get used to the way he talked, but I suppose a conversation with him was never boring, not when you didn't know what was coming next.

"When Matt asked me which one of him and his mates you fancied, I didn't tell them."

"Oh. Good," I said, feeling pretty relieved.

"But then I said you wouldn't fancy any of them, 'cause you were *way* too cool."

And with that, Dylan darted off, and immediately tripped over a speeding Kenneth.

I was glad that he was busy with trip-
ping, and that Soph and Fee were busy
with giggling and helping him up. That
way they couldn't see how much I was
blushing at the
excellent com-
pliment that
Dylan had just
given me.

He thought I was *way* cool!

Well, this week had been kind of weird, but by the end it had turned out kind of wonderful.

I might have thought I'd lost my best(est) friends, but in the end, I got them back, and a whole new one too!

(Uh-oh – when Dylan was getting himself back on his feet just now, did I see an **I ❤ MUM** logo popping up above his trainer…?)

the end